SCRAP'S ROBOTS

Be Overjoyed with a Droid!

SPRING CATALOG

DON'T DELAY! ORDER TODAY!
☎ PHONE 555 932 ROBOT

COOK-BOT
MODEL NO: 15642

WITHDRAWN FOR TECHNICAL REASONS

EAT!

YOU'LL NEVER DINE OUT AGAIN! WITH A COOK-BOT DELICIOUS MEALS FOR ALL! PASTA A SPECIALITY!

WASH-BOT
MODEL NO: 13986

WASH!

WITHDRAWN FOR TECHNICAL REASONS

TOO LAZY TO WASH? LET WASH-BOT SPONGE OFF YOUR FILTH & YOU WILL ALWAYS SMELL LIKE ROSES!

DRY-BOT
MODEL NO: 13278

WITHDRAWN FOR TECHNICAL REASONS

LATEST MODEL!

IS TOWELING YOURSELF A CHORE? LET DRY-BOT GENTLY BLOW THE DAMP FROM YOUR SKIN!

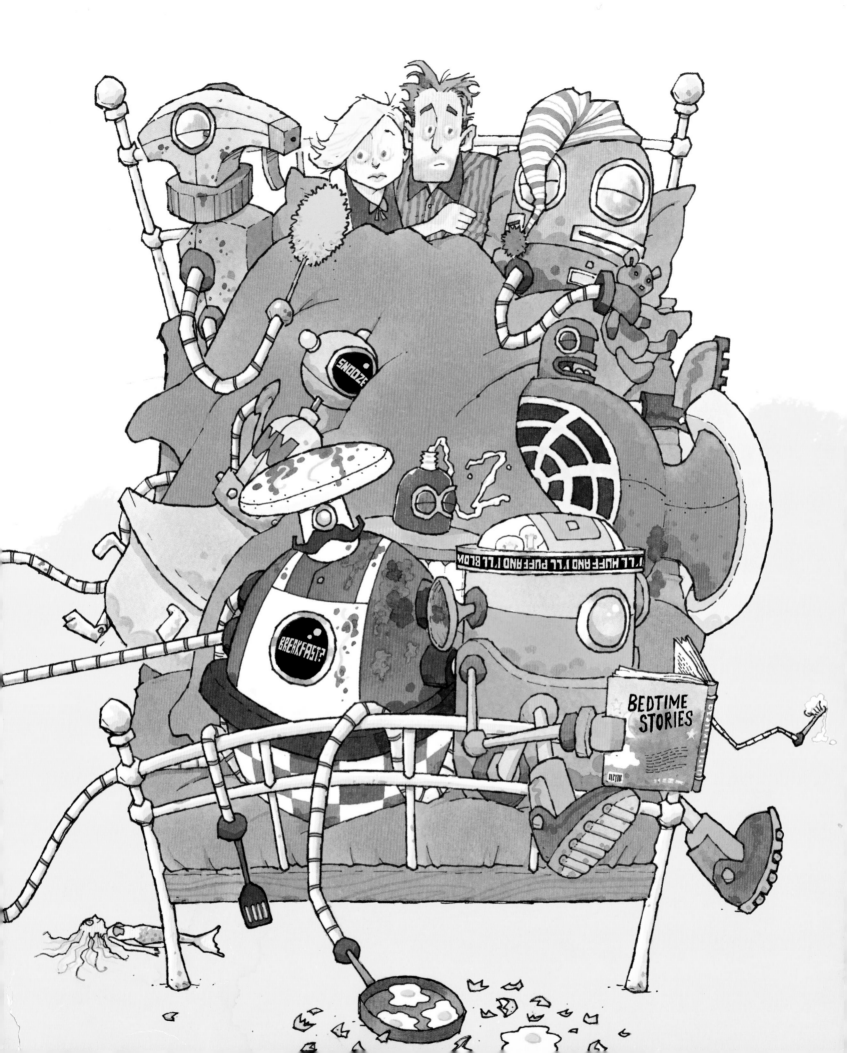

With
SEVEN ROBOTS
IN THEIR BED!

The place was a bit of a mess.
It hadn't worked quite like they'd said.
And I don't think they got a good night's sleep . . .

AAAARGH!!!!

I think the robots were exhausted.
They crashed around some more.
Then everything went quiet until . . .

So, in the end, I left them

and got **myself** into bed.

And Dry-bot couldn't manage to get my pajamas off its head.

Book-bot sat with a book on the bed,
and smoke coming out its ears.

I know that robots can't cry,
But Clean-bot looked close to tears.

I hoped it could sort out the mess.
This was getting beyond a laugh.
But all it did was cook more spaghetti
and tip it into the bath.

Cook-bot came in and stared.
And its warning-lights flashed too.
Then it nodded and zoomed away
like it knew just what to do.

But Dress-bot started putting pajamas on the robot that had to dry me.

Clean-bot was whizzing about.
It was trying to keep things tidy.

And Teeth-bot started brushing its head
and squirting toothpaste down the loo.

Dress-bot turned round and round like it didn't know what to do.

Then it went and slipped into Dress-bot,

who sat down on Teeth-bot's head.

It said, "DANGEROUS ANIMAL IN THE WATER!"

Three warning-lights flashed red.

Crocodile is my favorite toy.
His teeth can really snap.
But soon as Wash-bot spotted him,
it got in a bit of a flap.

Wash-bot ran a bath.

It said, "YOU WILL BE SPICK AND SPAN."

I got my bath toys down off the shelf.

But that's when the rumpus began.

Clean-bot did the washing-up.
Everything seemed just great.

Then Cook-bot made spaghetti.
I ate the lot off my plate.

I thought they must be joking.
But Dad switched the robots on.
Mum said, "They're the latest models.
What could *possibly* go wrong?"

My mum and dad are busy.
So just last night they said,
"We decided to buy these fantastic robots
to get you into bed."

For Fidelma and Tony – S.T.

For Hal & Ida – R.C.

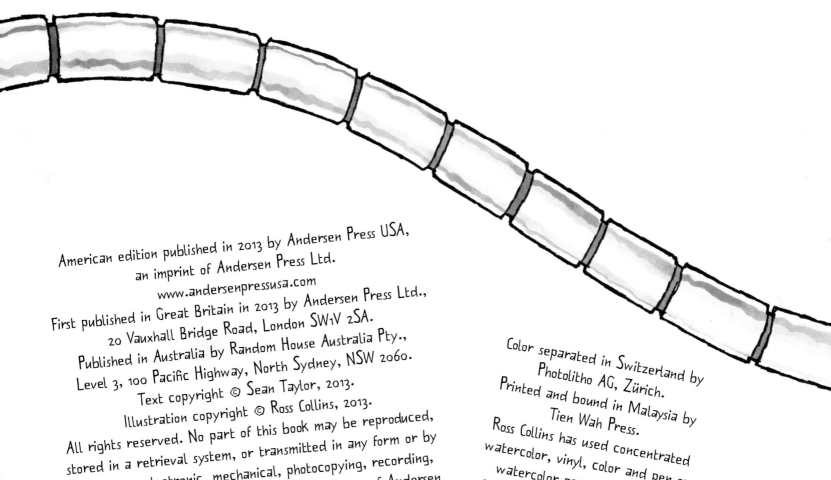

American edition published in 2013 by Andersen Press USA,
an imprint of Andersen Press Ltd.
www.andersenpressusa.com
First published in Great Britain in 2013 by Andersen Press Ltd.,
20 Vauxhall Bridge Road, London SW1V 2SA.
Published in Australia by Random House Australia Pty.,
Level 3, 100 Pacific Highway, North Sydney, NSW 2060.
Text copyright © Sean Taylor, 2013.
Illustration copyright © Ross Collins, 2013.

Distributed in the United States and Canada by
Lerner Publishing Group, Inc.
241 First Avenue North
Minneapolis, MN 55401 U.S.A.
www.lernerbooks.com

Color separated in Switzerland by
Photolitho AG, Zürich.
Printed and bound in Malaysia by
Tien Wah Press.
Ross Collins has used concentrated
watercolor, vinyl, color and pen on
watercolor paper in this book.
Library of Congress Cataloging-in-
Publication Data Available.
ISBN: 978-1-4677-2031-1
ISBN: 978-1-4677-2037-3 (eBook)
1 – TWP – 3/27/13

DRESS-BOT
MODEL NO: 15731

NEW!

GETTING DRESSED WAS NEVER SO EASY! DRESS-BOT STYLES YOUR OUTFITS FOR EVERY OCCASION!

CLEAN-BOT
MODEL NO: 12967

DIRTY DISHES? MESSY HOUSE? LIVE LIKE A PIG AND CLEAN-BOT WILL MAKE YOUR HOME SPARKLE!

BOOK-BOT
MODEL NO: 7372

TOO BUSY TO READ? LET BOOK-BOT READ FOR YOU! HEAR THE LATEST CLASSIC FROM SEAN TAYLOR!

TEETH-BOT
MODEL NO: 12087

NOW WITH FLOSSING! *

W9-AFG-720

TIRED OF BRUSHING YOUR GNASHERS? LET TEETH-BOT MAKE YOUR SMILE DAZZLE YOUR FRIENDS!